A T-Wit
for a
T-WOO

Layn Marlow

For A, the other half of my song – C F
For Theo and Angelika – so happy you found each other! – L M

ORCHARD BOOKS

First published in Great Britain in 2018
by The Watts Publishing Group

1 3 5 7 9 10 8 6 4 2

Text © Charlie Farley 2018
Illustrations © Layn Marlow 2018

The moral rights of the author and illustrator
have been asserted.

A CIP catalogue record for this book
is available from the British Library.

ISBN 978 1 40834 649 5

Printed and bound in China

FSC
www.fsc.org

MIX
Paper from
responsible sources
FSC® C104740

Orchard Books
An imprint of Hachette Children's Group
Part of The Watts Publishing Group Limited
Carmelite House
50 Victoria Embankment
London EC4Y 0DZ

An Hachette UK Company
www.hachette.co.uk
www.hachettechildrens.co.uk

A T-Wit
for a
T-WOO

Charlie Farley   Layn Marlow

ORCHARD

There once was an owl who lived in a wood,
Who wanted to do what every owl should.
He would fly each night through the wood that he loved,
And quietly gaze at the stars up above.

But something was missing that made him feel blue.
When he sang in the moonlight he'd just say, 'T-WOO!'
This sad little owl knew that something was wrong.
His **T-WOO** didn't sound like a proper owl song.

He'd heard other owls, far away in the night,
And they had an owl song, which sounded just right.
T-WIT...T-WOO! T-WIT...T-WOO!
they would call loud and clear.
Poor Twoo felt forlorn and he fought back a tear.

'I'm no good as an owl
if I've just a **T-WOO!**
I don't have a **T-WIT**,
oh, what shall I do?'

But then Twoo remembered
what Dad used to say,
'If you try your best son,
things will turn out okay'.

'I know I am little,' Twoo
thought, 'but I'm strong!
And I *will* find the other
half of my song.

I will search far-and-wide,
I'll give it my best,
I can do it! This will be my
true owl song quest!'

So our brave little Twoo flew into the night,
Determined to find what would make his song right.
He hadn't flown far, when out of the dark,
Came a beautiful sound that tugged at his heart.

'**T-WIT**,' came a call, then another, '**T-WIT**.'
Eyes wide with delight, Twoo thought, 'This is it!'
'**T-WOO!**' he replied, as he followed the call.
But now there was silence, no noise, none at all.

From treetop to treetop searched brave little Twoo,

Until out of the dark came a hullabaloo.

In a feathery flash, Twoo swooped through the air,

With hope in his heart that his **T-WIT** was down there.

But he just found badgers who said, 'Come and play.'
'I'd like to,' he sighed, 'though I really can't stay.
Did you hear that wonderful **T-WIT?**,' asked Twoo.
'No,' said the badgers, 'we only heard you.'

So on flew Twoo, further into the dark,
Till below him he spied dappled deer eating bark.
'I'm trying to find a T-WIT that I've heard.'

The deer all just blinked, 'No . . . we've not heard that word.
Just your funny **T-WOO** song, that sounds incomplete.
Ask the bats over there and leave us to eat.'

Twoo raced to the tree where the bats gently swayed,

Startling a family who looked most dismayed.

'Have you heard an owl song, a **T-WIT** for my **T-WOO?**'

'Nope,' said the dad bat, 'just noisy old you.

Be off with you! Find someone else to surprise.

Try Fox, he's so helpful and friendly and wise.'

Twoo began to believe he
would always be blue,
And Dad's, 'Try your best'
words might not be quite true.

Then Twoo saw the fox,
creeping past by itself,
Alone in the wood,
a picture of stealth.

'Mr. Fox,' called Twoo,
'are you all on your own?'
'I'm hunting,' said Fox,
'for my family back home.'
'Have you heard a **T-WIT**,
sounding something like me?'
'Hmmmm,' said the fox,
'Come down here, let me see.'

But as Twoo flew in closer – Fox's jaws opened wide . . .
It looked as if Twoo might end up inside.

Fox licked his lips . . .
'Oh, help!' Twoo cried.

Then suddenly pine cones rained down on all sides!

BUMP!
BUMP!
BUMP!

With a snarl and a yelp, sly Fox limped away.

No owl on the menu for this fox today!

Twoo sped to where help had come from on high.
'T-WIT,' came her call . . . 'T-WOO,' his reply.
And there on a branch a tawny owl stood,
In the light of the moon, in the dark of the wood.

'T-WIT,' she said shyly. 'T-WOO,' he blushed back.
From then on these two chose to follow one track.
She'd 'T-WIT,' and he'd 'T-WOO,' together each night,
Forever they'd keep one another in sight.

For now it was their wood,

their home, just these two,

And they lived there so happily,

Twit and her Twoo.

AUTHOR'S NOTE:

You see, the 'T-WIT T-WOO' of the

tawny owl is not one owl, but two . . .

A boy and a girl saying, 'How do you do.'